# Querido dragón va a la biblioteca

## Dear Dragon Goes to the Library

**por/by Margaret Hillert**

ilustrado por/Illustrated by David Schimmell

NORWOODHOUSE🏠PRESS

## Queridos padres y maestros:

La serie para lectores principiantes es una colección de lecturas cuidadosamente escritas, muchas de las cuales ustedes recordarán de su propia infancia. Cada libro comprende palabras de uso frecuente en español e inglés y, a través de la repetición, le ofrece al niño la oportunidad de practicarlas. Los detalles adicionales de las ilustraciones refuerzan la historia y le brindan la oportunidad de ayudar a su niño a desarrollar el lenguaje oral y la comprensión.

Primero, léale el cuento al niño; después deje que él lea las palabras con las que está familiarizado y pronto, podrá leer solito todo el cuento. En cada paso, elogie el esfuerzo del niño para que se sienta más confiado como lector independiente. Hable sobre las ilustraciones y anime al niño a relacionar el cuento con su propia vida.

Sobre todo, la parte más importante de la experiencia de la lectura es ¡divertirse y disfrutarla!

*Shannon Cannon*

Shannon Cannon
Consultora de lectoescritura

Norwood House Press • P.O. Box 316598 • Chicago, Illinois 60631
For more information about Norwood House Press please visit our website at
*www.norwoodhousepress.com* or call 866-565-2900.
Text copyright ©2010 by Margaret Hillert. Illustrations and cover design copyright ©2010 by Norwood House Press, Inc. All rights reserved. No part of this book may be reproduced or utilized in any form or by any means without written permission from the publisher.
Designer: The Design Lab

**LIBRARY OF CONGRESS CATALOGING-IN-PUBLICATION DATA**

Hillert, Margaret.
  [Dear dragon goes to the library. Spanish & English]
  Querido dragon va a la biblioteca = Dear dragon goes to the library / por Margaret Hillert ; ilustrado por David Schimmell ; traducido por Eida Del Risco.
       p. cm. — (A beginning-to-read book)
  Summary: "A boy and his pet dragon go to story time and take out books from the library. Carefully translated to include Spanish and English text"—Provided by publisher.
  ISBN-13: 978-1-59953-361-2 (library edition : alk. paper)
  ISBN-10: 1-59953-361-8 (library edition : alk. paper)
  [1. Dragons—Fiction. 2. Libraries—Fiction. 3. Books and reading—Fiction. 4. Spanish language materials—Bilingual.] I. Schimmell, David, ill. II. Del Risco, Eida. III. Title. IV. Title: Dear dragon goes to the library.

  PZ73.H557211 2010
  [E]—dc22

                          2009041514
Manufactured in the United States of America in North Mankato, Minnesota.
                          180R-042011

Ven. Ven.
Quiero que me ayudes.
Quiero que vayas
a un lugar conmigo.

Come here. Come here.
I want you to help me.
I want you to go
somewhere with me.

Quiero este
y este
y este
y este.

I want this
and this
and this
and this.

El rojo
y el azul
y el amarillo.

The red one
and the blue one
and the yellow one.

Ayúdame con esto.
Ahora nos podemos ir.
Tenemos que caminar y caminar.

Help me with this.
We can go now.
We have to walk and walk.

Mira allá. Mira eso.
Allí es donde queremos ir.

Look there. See that.
That is where we want to go.

7

Es bueno venir aquí.
Ya verás.
Es un buen lugar.

It is good to go here.
You will see.
It is a good spot.

8

Tenemos que subir.
Arriba, arriba, arriba.
Tú lo puedes hacer.

We have to go up here.
Up, up, up.
You can do it.

¿Qué es esto?
Parece divertido. Lo quiero ver.

What is this?
This looks like fun. I want to see this.

Mira aquí. Mira a los niños y a las niñas.
A ellos les gusta estar ahí.

Look in here. See the boys and girls.
They like it there.

Nosotros podemos entrar también,
pero tienes que portarte bien.

We can come in here, too,
but you have to be good.

¿Adónde podemos ir ahora?
¿Qué podemos hacer?

Where can we go now?
What can we do?

¿Qué hay aquí?
Parece algo divertido.
Lo quiero hacer.

What is in here?
This looks like fun.
I want to do this.

Huy. Mira esto. Se parece a ti.

Oh, my. Look at this. It looks like you.

Y aquí también hay algo que hacer.

And here is something to do, too.

Puedo hacer esto.
Uno, dos, tres.
Es divertido hacerlo.

I can do this—
One—two—three.
It is fun to do this.

Pero ahora tenemos que recoger algo e irnos.

But now we have to get something and we have to go.

Quiero el que se parece a ti.
Y quiero este rojo
y el azul y el amarillo.

I want the one that looks like you.
And I want this red one,
and the blue one, and the yellow one.

Y este también parece bueno.
Bueno, bueno, ¡BUENO!

And this one looks good.
Good, good, GOOD!

Ahí vamos.
Mamá se va a poner contenta cuando nos vea.

Here we go.
Mother will be happy to see us.

Mamá, mamá. Mira.
Tenemos algo bueno.

Mother, Mother. Look here.
We have something good.

Tú estás conmigo
y yo estoy contigo.
Ay, qué libro más bueno, querido dragón.

Here you are with me.
And here I am with you.
Oh, what a good book, dear dragon.

28

Here i...
It f...

Ll

The following activities support the findings of the National Reading Panel that determined the most effective components for reading instruction are: Phonemic Awareness, Phonics, Vocabulary, Fluency, and Text Comprehension.

## Phonemic Awareness: Plurals

1. Explain to your child that when a word stands for more than one of something, it is called a plural and that the /s/ sound is added to the word to make it plural. Say the following singular words aloud and ask your child to respond with the plural form:

| | | |
|---|---|---|
| boy=boys | dragon=dragons | book=books |
| wagon=wagons | stair=stairs | puzzle=puzzles |
| kid=kids | bear=bears | chair=chairs |

2. Read the plural forms of each word and ask your child to respond with the singular form.

## Phonics: Plural Spelling for Words Ending in consonant+y

1. Turn to page 9 and point to the name on the building and read the word library.

2. Ask your child to name the final letter in the word library (y).

3. Ask your child to say the plural word for more than one library (libraries).

4. Fold a sheet of paper in half lengthwise. Draw a line down the center of the paper. Write the word library at the top of the left column and the word libraries at the top of the right column.

5. Ask your child to notice which letters are the same and which letters are different in the two words.

6. Explain to your child that when a singular word ends in a consonant plus **-y**, we need to change the **y** to an **i** and add the letters **es** to make it plural.

7. Write the following words in the left column:

| | | | | |
|---|---|---|---|---|
| story | baby | puppy | mommy | pony |
| family | daisy | lady | party | daddy |

8. Read each word aloud and ask your child to repeat it.

9. Ask your child to write the plural form of each noun in the right-hand column. Remind your child that she or he needs to change the **y** to an **i** and add **es**.

## Vocabulary: Physical Science/Force Words

1. Turn to page 7. Ask your child what the boy is doing (pushing the wagon). Ask your child what the dragon is doing (pulling the wagon).

2. Write the word **push** at the top of a blank sheet of paper and the word **pull** at the top of another blank sheet of paper.

3. Ask your child to draw things that can be pushed on the paper labeled **push** and things that can be pulled on the paper labeled **pull**.

4. Ask your child to name the drawings and label each one.

5. Ask your child to make a complete sentence using the illustrations and labels. (For example: I can pull a wagon.)

6. Examples of pushes and pulls:

   Push: swing, chair toward the table, door closed, lawnmower, shopping cart, baby stroller, doorbell, pedals on a bicycle

   Pull: rope, chair away from the table, door opened, socks on feet, sled, trailer, a weed from the ground, picking fruit from a tree

## Fluency: Shared Reading

1. Reread the story to your child at least two more times while your child tracks the print by running a finger under the words as they are read. Ask your child to read the words he or she knows with you.

2. Reread the story taking turns, alternating readers between sentences or pages.

## Text Comprehension: Discussion Time

1. Ask your child to retell the sequence of events in the story.

2. To check comprehension, ask your child the following questions:

   • Where did the boy and the dragon go?

   • What happened when they were there?

   • What kinds of books would you like to check out from the library?

Margaret Hillert ha escrito más de 80 libros para niños que están aprendiendo a leer. Sus libros han sido traducidos a muchos idiomas y han sido leídos por más de un millón de niños de todo el mundo. De niña, Margaret empezó escribiendo poesía y más adelante siguió escribiendo para niños y adultos. Durante 34 años, fue maestra de primer grado. Ya se retiró, y ahora vive en Michigan donde le gusta escribir, dar paseos matinales y cuidar a sus tres gatos.

Photograph by Glenna Washburn

**ABOUT THE AUTHOR**

Margaret Hillert has written over 80 books for children who are just learning to read. Her books have been translated into many different languages and over a million children throughout the world have read her books. She first started writing poetry as a child and has continued to write for children and adults throughout her life. A first grade teacher for 34 years, Margaret is now retired from teaching and lives in Michigan where she likes to write, take walks in the morning, and care for her three cats.

**ACERCA DEL ILUSTRADOR**

David Schimmell fue bombero durante 23 años, al cabo de los cuales guardó las botas y el casco y se dedicó a trabajar como ilustrador. David ha creado las ilustraciones para la nueva serie de Querido dragón, así como para muchos otros libros. David nació y se crió en Evansville, Indiana, donde aún vive con su esposa, dos hijos, un nieto y dos nietas.

**ABOUT THE ILLUSTRATOR**

David Schimmell served as a professional firefighter for 23 years before hanging up his boots and helmet to devote himself to work as an illustrator. David has happily created the illustrations for the New Dear Dragon books as well as many other books throughout his career. Born and raised in Evansville, Indiana, he lives there today with his wife, two sons, a grandson and two granddaughters.